# Mum goes to work

Libby Gleeson
& Leila Rudge

WALKER BOOKS
AND SUBSIDIARIES

LONDON • BOSTON • SYDNEY • AUCKLAND

It's early morning.

Everyone is arriving at the centre.

It's noisy and busy while

Mark and Mai greet everyone.

Mum is going to work.

"Bye, Mum."

"Bye."

Nadia's mother is a student.
She goes to classes and
then reads in the library.

She writes in a folder
and talks with the teacher
about her work.

Nadia paints a picture for her mum.

Then she and Jack build a city in the block corner. It takes a very long time.

Laurence's mother works in a cafe. She shows the customers a menu. Then she takes the orders to the kitchen and brings the food to the customers.

When they are finished she collects their money to pay the bill.

Laurence and Georgia
play in the sandpit.

They make a three-layer
sand cake and lots of
sand biscuits.
Then they play on the
swing that hangs from
the tree house.

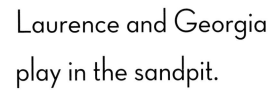

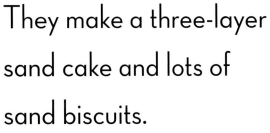

Max's mother is a nurse.
She gives the patients
their medicine and makes
them comfortable.

She checks all
the machines
and talks to the
doctor about each
sick person.

Max plays in the
dressing-up corner.

He and Ann put the dolls to bed,
and then join the others
for music and a story.

Rosie and Jack's mother works
at home with their new baby.
She feeds and baths him.
While he's sleeping, she sorts
the laundry and tidies the house.

Later she takes him shopping
in the pram.

Rosie, Jack and Nadia
wash all the dolls and teddies
and put them out to dry.
They empty the water onto
the dirt and make a big mud pie.

Then it's time to scrub
their hands and sit down to lunch.

After lunch it's quiet time.

Mai pats Louis to sleep.

Georgia's and Louis's mothers work for the council.

Georgia's mother is a gardener. She plants all the flowerbeds in the park.

Louis's mother is at the front desk.

She helps anyone who comes in with a problem.

Georgia and Louis wake up from their sleep and give Mark a cuddle.

They go out and water the vegetable patch and pick some flowers.

They each make a long pasta necklace for their mothers.

Ann's mother works in a clothes shop.
She unpacks the new T-shirts and
puts them on the shelves.

She helps the customers find the clothes
that they like best and that fit them well.

Ann and Ali empty the ragbag on the floor.

They stick different pieces on the big sheet of paper to hang on the wall.

Then they put together the brightly coloured puzzles.

Brigit's mother works in an office.

She turns on her computer and answers the emails.

Then she makes a coffee and takes it to a meeting in a different room.

Later she writes a report on the computer.

Brigit and Max make a computer
each from some boxes.
They draw on lots of numbers
and buttons.

When they finish they help Mai
cut up apples and celery for
afternoon tea.

Ali's mother is a teacher.
She reads to her class.

Then she helps the children
write their own stories.

After they go home
she prepares work
for the next morning.

Ali and Brigit help Mark put the bikes away.

Then Ali takes all the dolls and the teddies into the quiet corner and shows them some picture books.

It's nearly time to go home. Everyone is feeling tired.

"See you tomorrow."

"Bye."